W9-CEH-740

NANCY CLANCY
Seeks a Fortune

BOOK 7

NANCY CLANCY

Seeks a Fortune

WRITTEN BY
Jane O'Connor

ILLUSTRATIONS BY
Robin
Preiss Glasser

HARPER
An Imprint of HarperCollins*Publishers*

Library of Congress Control Number: 2015952522
ISBN 978-0-06-226969-0

Typography by Jeanne L. Hogle
16 17 18 19 20   CG/RRDH   10 9 8 7 6 5 4 3
❖
First Edition

For Robin Preiss Glasser—

how fortunate that we became a pair!

—J.O'C.

For Beth and Georgie,

with all my love forever

—R.P.G.

CONTENTS

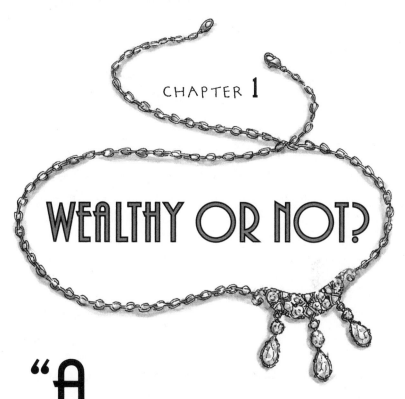

CHAPTER 1

WEALTHY OR NOT?

"Are we wealthy?" Nancy asked her parents. Being wealthy sounded—well, it sounded wealthier than just being rich.

It was Sunday afternoon. Her father was checking the kitchen cabinets and making out a grocery list. Her mother sat at the breakfast table, paying bills. JoJo was feeding Frenchy part of a sugar cookie.

Her mom looked up from her laptop. "What makes you ask that?"

"Mom!" Nancy cried. "You always do that!"

"Do what?" her mom asked.

"Instead of answering a question, you ask another one." Nancy sighed. "I'm not being nosy. I am being inquisitive. So . . . are we?"

"Nope," her mother said. "We're definitely not wealthy."

"But," her dad added, "we have a roof over our heads that only leaks a little, clothes on our backs, and—once I get back from the supermarket—I can promise none of us will go hungry."

"Exactly. We aren't rich and we aren't poor." Nancy's mother handed her father a bunch of coupons for stuff on sale. "We are lucky to be somewhere in the middle," she told Nancy. "We have everything we need but maybe not everything we wish we had."

Nancy had expected that answer. The Clancys were average. That was fine. She understood that her family was lucky not to be poor. Still, average sounded boring.

"Grace's family is wealthy."

Nancy's mom didn't answer. She was focused on her laptop.

"Her grandpa is a millionaire," Nancy went on. "Someday Grace will be an heiress. That means she'll get tons of money after he's dead."

Getting a fortune sounded great to Nancy. Finding a fortune sounded even better. At school, room 3D was learning about the Gold Rush of 1849.

"Did you know that as soon as gold was found in California, thousands and thousands of people raced out there? They all wanted to find gold and get rich quick, and some did!" Nancy paused, then went on, "If that happened to me, we could fly to Paris and stay at a fancy hotel. I'd buy a whole new wardrobe. Not

just for me but for all of you."

"Merci beaucoup," her mom said. "That's very sweet." Then she put down a stack of bills. "Sure, being rich would be fun. Still, it isn't what's most important to Dad or me."

Her dad stuffed the shopping list and coupons in his back pocket. Then he jangled his car keys. "Come on, girls. After the Stop and Shop we can hit a tag sale.

Who knows what treasures we'll find."

Nancy knew that by "treasures" her dad meant old superhero comic books. He had boxes and boxes of them from when he was a kid. And he was always adding to his collection.

JoJo leaped up on their dad for a piggyback ride out the door.

"Alas, I cannot come," Nancy told her father. She had to put the finishing touches on her project for Gold Fever Day. It was tomorrow. And Nancy's project was superb, if she did say so herself.

CHAPTER 2

TREASURE HUNTING

I t was late afternoon. Nancy finished gluing gold glitter and pebbles to the bottom of an old pie pan. The pebbles were painted gold. Then she started writing her paragraph. She stuck in as many vivid—that meant interesting— words as she could think of.

"Long ago in days of yore, one way prospectors discovered gold was by—"

Suddenly a bell rang outside her window. It meant Bree had sent a message in their Top-Secret Special Delivery mailbox. The mailbox was actually a basket. It was strung on a rope between Nancy's bedroom window and Bree's.

Nancy reeled in the basket and looked at the message. It was written in secret code. The trouble was, she and Bree kept switching codes to make sure their messages stayed super-secret. Which code were they using now? It took a minute before it came to her. She had to look at each letter and then jump back to the one before it in the alphabet. B became A, C became B, and so on.

The message was brief. It said: *Meet me in the clubhouse. Now!*

Ooh la la! This sounded important, maybe even urgent. Finishing her homework would just have to wait!

Nancy dashed downstairs and out the side door into the Clancys' backyard. She had just plopped down on one of the beanbag chairs in the clubhouse when Bree came bursting in.

"Ta-da!" she cried, and thrust an arm out toward Nancy. Bree was holding a long black rod with a big double ring on one end.

"What on earth is that contraption?" Nancy asked.

"A metal detector."

A metal detector? Nancy sprang from the beanbag chair to take a closer look.

"My dad needed to rent one for a commercial he's shooting. For Solid Gold chocolate bars." Bree's father worked at an advertising agency. He did way more fun stuff than Nancy's father, who helped people with their taxes. "We can try it out if we're careful."

"For real?" Nancy clutched Bree's hand.

"Who knows? We might find long-lost treasure!"

"Fingers crossed!" Bree wanted to get

rich quick just as much as Nancy did. But she was more realistic. So she said, "Look, it'll be exciting if we just find some coins. Watch this." Bree pushed a button at the top of the rod. Then she pointed the

double-ring thingie at the buckles on her shoes.

Bleep! Bleep! Bleep! went the metal detector.

Double ooh la la! "Do it on me now!" Nancy bent down so Bree could point the double rings at the silver barrettes in Nancy's hair.

The metal detector bleeped wildly again!

They didn't bother shooting to see who got to look for treasure first. Since the metal detector belonged to Bree, sort of, it seemed only fair to start in her yard. And it went without saying that any treasure they found they'd split even Stephen.

They began at the far end of the yard by the fence. Slowly they worked their way toward the deck. The metal detector was much heavier than it looked. So they took turns, walking in straight lines back and forth, back and forth, across the grass.

The metal detector didn't bleep a lot. But every time it did, the girls searched carefully to see what had set it off. After an hour, they had found:

- a key
- a bent spoon
- the top of a tuna-fish can
- a penny

"Maybe the key opens a treasure chest that's buried somewhere," Nancy said, but she didn't sound very convincing, not even to herself.

"Nancy, face it. It's a house key. That's all." Bree handed over the metal detector.

"Maybe we'll have better luck in your yard."

In Nancy's yard pretty much the same kind of stuff turned up. Only a fork instead of a spoon and not even a single penny.

By now the sun was low in the sky.

It was almost dinnertime. Nancy walked Bree back home. They took the shortcut, squeezing through the tall bushes separating their yards.

Suddenly the metal detector bleeped once more. Not very loudly.

"It won't turn out to be anything good," Bree said.

Still, they both knelt in the dirt and felt around with their hands.

Nancy touched something first. Her fingers wrapped around a very thin chain. Nancy gave a gentle tug and—triple ooh la la!—suddenly a very grubby necklace was in the palm of her hand.

Bree and Nancy both let out a scream.

"It's the one Mrs. DeVine gave you!" Bree exclaimed. "The one you lost."

Indeed it was. For once Nancy was speechless. She had never expected to lay eyes on the necklace again.

Nancy had often admired the necklace,

19

which Mrs. DeVine kept in a jewelry box, and then—surprise, surprise—Mrs. DeVine presented it to Nancy on her last birthday. The necklace was more than fifty years old. Mrs. DeVine said it was a piece of costume jewelry. That meant the sparkly teardrops were rhinestones, not real diamonds. Nancy didn't care. It was like wearing a tiny chandelier around her neck. Then a month ago the necklace had gone missing.

After rubbing off more dirt, Nancy could see that the clasp on the chain didn't close all the way. That explained how it had gotten lost.

"I never even told Mrs. DeVine. I felt so bad. I thought it was my fault—that I'd been careless. But I wasn't!"

"Wear it tonight when we go over to her house."

Nancy smacked her forehead. *"Sacre bleu!"* That was French for yikes. "I totally forgot."

On Sunday night *Antiques in Your Attic* was on TV. Bree and Nancy always went to Mrs. DeVine's to watch it. Every week people brought in stuff from home and had it appraised. That meant they found out what it was worth. Most of the time stuff that looked like junk was just junk. But once in a while a super-ugly vase or a painting of crazy blobs turned out to be really valuable. That was always so thrilling to see. One woman fainted right on TV after hearing the good news.

Sunday night counted as a school night,

21

of course. However, Bree and Nancy were allowed to watch the show since it was on public TV and counted as educational . . . but only if all their homework was done.

"I haven't finished the writing part of my Gold Fever project." Actually Nancy had hardly begun it. "I may have to miss the show."

"Nan-cy!" Bree sounded irritated. She never left homework for the last minute. Never, ever.

At that very moment the girls heard Nancy's mother calling her home for dinner. *Antiques in Your Attic* would be coming on right after that.

"Maybe I can finish in time to see the end of the show," Nancy said.

As she walked back to her house, Nancy

told herself that even if she got stuck doing homework, finding the necklace was worth missing TV. Although she hadn't found any long-lost treasure today, she had found recently lost treasure.

That was just as superb.

CHAPTER 3

SUNDAY NIGHT TV

"Nancy! You won't believe this!" Bree exclaimed. "You just missed a lady with an old doll. It was naked and missing an arm. But it was worth two thousand dollars!"

"Sacre bleu!" Nancy said as she entered the living room and took a seat on the

divan. That's what Mrs. DeVine called the couch.

"Have a cookie." Mrs. DeVine passed a tray of fancy cookies to Nancy. "Oh! I see you're wearing your necklace."

Nancy touched her throat. Her mom had fixed the clasp. Even so, Nancy had put tape around it. She wasn't taking any chances.

"The lady got the doll at a tag sale," Bree went on. "She only paid fifty cents. Nancy, it was so creepy-looking, I had to shut my eyes." Bree paused and gave a little shudder. "When the lady heard what it was worth, her eyes bugged way out and she said . . ."

"Wait! Let me guess," Nancy shouted. "I bet she said, 'Wow! Are you kidding? I had no idea!'"

It was what everybody said. Every single time.

The TV program was almost over.

A kid brought in a wind-up toy bank. It had once belonged to his great-grandfather. After he put a penny on the seal's nose and turned a key in its back, the penny flipped way up and then dropped down into the slot in the bank.

"That's pretty awesome," Nancy said. Then she corrected herself. "I mean to say, 'That's startling and unusual!'" Her teacher, Mr. Dudeny, thought that "awesome" was a boring word because kids used it way too much.

"Ooh, guess what." Bree brushed a cookie crumb off her upper lip. "The penny I found was old. From 1956. It looks

 different from pennies now. There's a picture of wheat on the back side. So I called Grace."

"Grace is a girl in our class," Nancy explained to Mrs. DeVine. "She says she's a coin expert."

"Well, Grace called me back. Her coin book said that the penny might be worth as much as a nickel."

"Girls. Girls. Pay attention. This looks interesting." Mrs. DeVine was pointing at her TV.

A young couple had brought a statue of an angel. They had bought it on their honeymoon in Europe. "I collect angels," the wife said. "And I had to have this one. It cost a lot and my husband thought I was

crazy to pay so much. But the owner of the shop promised it was from the Middle Ages. It's wood and some of the paint is still on it. See?" She pointed to the angel's wooden curls.

"Do you mind my asking how much you paid?" the TV show woman asked.

"Six . . . hundred . . . dollars." The husband spoke each word separately and slowly. Nancy almost expected him to start twirling a finger around his ear. She could tell that he thought spending six hundred dollars was cuckoo-cuckoo.

"Uh-oh. This isn't looking good," Mrs. DeVine said. "Look at the appraiser's face. I think the wife got swindled." Mrs. DeVine explained that meant the lady had been lied to and paid way too much.

Mrs. DeVine was 100 percent correct.

The appraiser looked sad and said, "I am afraid this object was made to appear old, but it's not. The wood is new wood. And the paint on the angel is modern-day paint. Not the kind that artists in the Middle Ages used." The appraiser

said that the angel was still very pretty—
"decorative" was the word she used. Then
she delivered the bad news. "I'm so sorry
to tell you that this statue is worth less
than a hundred dollars."

"I—I don't care. I still—s-still love it,"
the wife stammered. But you could tell
her husband did care.

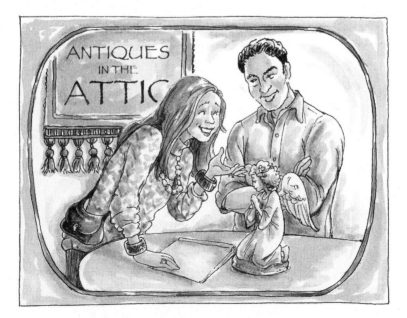

"I think that couple with the angel is having a *big* fight right about now." Mrs. DeVine stretched out the word "big."

Nancy and Bree both agreed.

"Maybe they'll show up on *Divorce Court*," Nancy said, and giggled. That was another of Mrs. DeVine's favorite shows but not one that the girls were allowed to watch.

A minute later the program ended with the host asking home viewers to "check the show's website to see if *Antiques in Your Attic* is coming to your town."

Nancy and Bree stood and thanked Mrs. DeVine. They kissed Jewel on the top of her head. Tonight she had on a tiny gold tiara. . . . *Très* fancy!

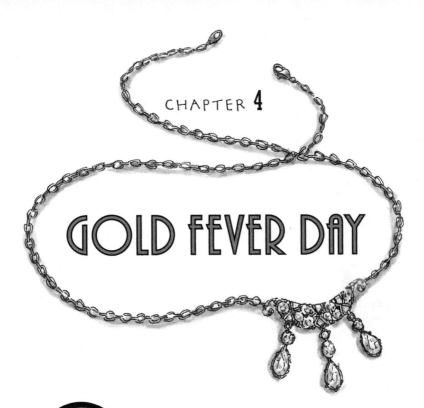

CHAPTER **4**

GOLD FEVER DAY

O n Monday morning, a surprise was waiting for everyone in 3D. Mr. Dudeny was growing a beard.

"What made you do it?" Nancy asked.

"To tell the truth, I got tired of shaving every morning."

"Same here, dude," Lionel said. He had

35

a beard too. Of course, his was a fake one. Along with the beard, he was wearing a pair of old overalls and a bandanna around his neck. Lionel explained that he was supposed to look like an old-time miner from the days of the Gold Rush. So when classed started, Mr. D called on Lionel first to tell everyone about his project.

"This here rock is called pyrite," Lionel began, and held up a big chunk of something gold-colored and sparkling. He passed it around the class.

"Pyrite looks like real gold, don't it? Sure had me fooled. That's why they call it fool's gold. Miners like me would find a big piece and start shouting that we had struck it rich. But pyrite ain't worth nothin'." Then Lionel whipped off his bandanna and began sobbing into it.

Grace went next. She showed the class a tiny coin inside a little plastic envelope. Her millionaire grandpa had given it to her.

"That's the smallest coin I've ever seen," Robert said, squinting at it. "It makes a dime look big."

Grace looked not mad, exactly, but

annoyed. "For your information, this happens to be real gold," she said. "Not fake like pyrite." Then Grace told the class about her coin collection. "This one is nearly a hundred years old and it's worth tons of money. Tons."

Maybe so. But Nancy didn't see how the coin had much to do with the Gold Rush except that it was gold. She turned to Bree and they exchanged looks. *Show-off!* they were both thinking. Being best friends meant that they could often read each other's minds.

After Grace, it was Robert's turn. He had drawn a big map of the US. It showed how wagon trains made their way across the country to California.

Bree went next. "I made an ad like the

ones that used to run in newspapers." In very big, very neat letters, Bree had written, *Get rich quick! Come to California. There's gold in those hills. And it can be yours!*

"People would read ads like this and rush out West. But not many found gold. So it's really false advertising," Bree explained before sitting down.

As Mr. Dudeny looked around the room to choose who would go next, Nancy figured he might call on her since she sat next to Bree. But instead he said, "Clara, I'm really anxious to know what's under the napkin in your basket. Something sure smells good."

It turned out to be biscuits.

"I took out a book from the library . . . ,"

Clara began in a soft voice. Almost a whisper.

Mr. Dudeny asked her to start over. "Remember. Loud and proud, Clara!"

Clara cleared her throat. "Well, in my library book, it said that one time a miner in a camp saw a lady from another tent baking biscuits. He was so hungry for something good to eat that he paid her ten dollars for one biscuit. But you can all have one for free. It's my grandma Bee's recipe and it's really good."

"That is absolutely superb information," Mr. Dudeny told her.

Clara beamed. Then she passed out her biscuits. She also had brought in a jar of strawberry jam.

Nancy smeared some over her biscuit and took a bite. Ooh la la. Yummy! Delectable! Scrumptious.

Mr. Dudeny was looking at the wall clock. "I think we have time to hear from one more person. How about you, Miss Clancy?"

Enfin! (In French that meant "At last!") Nancy stood. She had a bottle of water, a plastic bowl, and the pie pan. It was filled with dirt and gravel from her driveway.

"One way miners in California found gold was by looking in streams," she told the class. "They called it panning because they used a pan. Sometimes it was the same pan they used for cooking. They'd scoop up some gravel and water." Nancy paused to pour water into the pie pan. "Gold is heavier than water or dirt or gravel, so any gold sank to the bottom. Prospectors—that's another name for miners—would swirl their pans around

until all the water and other stuff ran out. And sometimes . . ." Slowly Nancy drained all the water and gravel into the plastic bowl. "*Voilà!* There'd be gold!"

She tilted the pie pan so everyone could see the glittering bottom.

"Cool!" said a few kids. But after Nancy handed Mr. D her paragraph and took her seat, she couldn't help feeling a little let down. She had worked pretty hard on her project and it was good. But it wasn't superb. Not like biscuits.

CHAPTER **5**

GETTING RICH QUICK

Nancy and Bree were not the only kids in 3D trying to get rich quick. Everybody was—everybody except Grace. "I don't need to," she said. "I'm already rich."

Later that week, Lionel brought in something he called "Insta-Beard." Wads of cotton balls, painted brown, were glued on the end

of a stick—the flat kind that doctors used when you had to open wide and say "Aah." Lionel showed it around the cafeteria.

"Insta-Beard!" he said. "This is going to be the next big fad. Like Pet Rocks."

Tamar looked up from her sandwich. "Pet what?" she asked.

"Pet Rocks. They were a fad in the seventies," Bree piped in. "My dad still has his. It was a rock you pretended was a puppy. It came with a book on how to feed and care for your pet rock."

"A pet rock." Clara giggled. "That's so dumb."

Lionel was nodding. "That was the point. The guy who thought it up made millions." Lionel popped his Insta-Beard in front of his mouth.

Clara giggled again, but Nancy thought she was mostly doing it to be nice. Pet Rocks were dumb but funny. To Nancy, the fake beard just looked kind of dumb.

"I can turn these out really fast." Then Lionel told the kids something that Nancy already knew. His mom was a dentist. "I have a box of tongue depressors at home. Cotton balls too. . . . We can all look like Mr. D."

"I liked him better without the beard," Nola confessed, and everyone else at the table nodded in agreement.

Sadly for Lionel, Insta-Beard was a flop.

During recess he showed his sample beard around. He tried to get orders from younger kids. A first-grade boy seemed interested until he heard the price.

"A dollar? No way," he told Lionel.

"As a special introductory offer, I'll charge only seventy-five cents."

The kid shook his head and ran off to join a game of dodgeball.

At recess the next day, other new businesses opened. Grace was selling old coins. Ones she had doubles or triples of.

"Wait a minute. You told us you didn't need to get rich," Nancy said.

"So? It can't hurt to get richer," Grace replied. She tried selling Nancy a penny with a picture of wheat on the back side. "It'll cost you a dime."

Bree heard Grace and said, "Oh, no! You told me the one I found was only worth a nickel, tops. It has the same stalks of wheat on it."

Grace scowled. "Well—well, this one is shiny and looks new. You said yours was all dirty."

Nancy was already backing away. Was Grace trying to swindle her? *"Merci, mais non merci,"* Nancy said. In French it meant, "Thanks, but no thanks."

On the other side of the yard, Nola was selling baseball cards. She had a huge stack. A crowd of kids surrounded her. It looked like she was doing pretty good business until Mr. Dudeny appeared. "Sorry, I'm closing down this operation." Then he went over to Grace and made her put away the coins.

"Dudes. Recess is for running around, playing games, or just spacing out for forty minutes if that's what you want to do," he said once everybody was back at their desks. He scratched his beard. He'd been doing that a lot. Clearly he wasn't used to so much hair on his face. "Not

that I don't admire your entrepreneurial spirit."

"Our what?" Yoko asked.

"Entrepreneurial spirit. An entrepreneur is someone who comes up with a smart idea to make money. You say it like this— on-truh-prenn-ur. It's a French word." As he said this Mr. D smiled at Nancy. He knew Nancy Clancy was absolutely crazy about everything French.

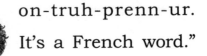

"Everything starts with an idea," Mr. Dudeny went on.

"Some ideas don't work."

"Yeah, tell me about it," Lionel said. He couldn't give away his Insta-Beards for free.

"And some ideas are so superb they change the way we live. Telephones, airplanes, computers. They all started from an idea and people who simply refused to give up on their dream."

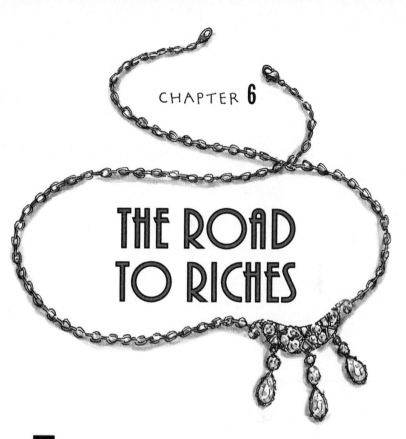

CHAPTER 6

THE ROAD TO RICHES

Even though school was off-limits, that didn't stop the entrepreneurs in 3D from coming up with new ideas for making a fortune.

Robert started offering lasso lessons at his house. He had once lived in Texas and knew lots of rope-twirling tricks. Five kids signed up right away.

Yoko invited kids over to show them the bead jewelry she'd made. She wanted to sell it. She didn't get many orders. Most of the girls already made the same kind of bracelets themselves.

Clara's business was the biggest success. She opened a biscuit stand. Nancy and Bree saw it on Saturday when they biked by her house.

"I'm doing great!" Clara said, and gave them each a free biscuit.

"You have a wonderful product," Bree told her.

"Simply delectable," agreed Nancy, wiping biscuit crumbs from her lips.

"What's wrong with us?" Nancy asked

Bree when they were back at the club-house. "Everybody else is making money."

Bree was sprawled on the beanbag chair. "We just have to figure out what we're great at that nobody else is."

They pondered awhile. That meant they were thinking really hard.

"We have the most superb fashion sense," Nancy pointed out.

Bree agreed but said, "Who will pay us to tell them what clothes to wear?"

"Well, we know how to make the most of our natural beauty," Nancy said. "What if we opened a spa?"

"Where? Here in the clubhouse?" At first Bree looked excited. But then she shook her head. "There's a real spa in town. Who'd come to ours?"

Nancy frowned. Bree was right.

Then Bree sat up straighter. "But we could sell homemade beauty products!"

"Like for skin care?"

"Sure. Why not!"

Bree and Nancy high-fived each other. Then they dashed over to Nancy's house. In the den, Nancy turned on her mom's laptop.

"Recipes for homemade skin cream," they typed into a search engine.

In five minutes they had copied down one. They needed vanilla yogurt, honey, and nutmeg.

"I'm pretty sure we have all the stuff. Let's check in the kitchen."

Luckily Nancy's dad had bought the wrong yogurt—vanilla, not plain—for a meatball dish he was making for dinner.

"Sure. Take it," he said. When he heard what it was for, he rubbed his jaw. "Softer skin? Put me down for a jar."

Ooh la la! Their first customer!

The only ingredient missing was nutmeg.

"How important can that be? We only have to use a half teaspoon." Nancy was searching through the spice rack. "We have cinnamon. You think that'll work?"

"Probably," Bree said. "Anyway, we shouldn't copy the recipe exactly. It has to be our special secret formula."

While Nancy and Bree whipped up their first batch, they discussed names for their skin cream. Nancy wanted something French. So she wiped her hands on a paper towel and went to find the Clancys' French-English dictionary. A few moments later— *voilà*—they came up with a superb

name . . . Crème Secrète. It meant secret cream.

Back in the kitchen, Bree poured the glop into clean jam jars. "All that work and we only filled three."

"We can make bigger batches once the orders come in," Nancy said.

Bree picked up one of the jars. "We need a great label. My dad says that's really important if you want your product to sell." Then she snapped her fingers. "The gold wrappers!" She explained to Nancy that her dad had gotten a whole carton of Solid Gold chocolate bars. Bree had saved all the wrappers from ones she'd eaten. "They were too pretty to throw away!"

Over at Bree's house they made elegant gold foil labels, argued over the right price for Crème Secrète, settled on $2.99, and then decided to make a commercial.

"We can put it up on YouTube," Nancy said. "We'll email everybody we know and tell them to watch. Maybe it'll go viral!" A few months ago, a home movie of Nancy's act in the third-grade variety show had gone viral. Over a million people had watched it.

Before filming the commercial, they wrote out a script. Figuring out the beginning was simple. It went like this:

"People often compliment me on my youthful, petal-soft complexion. I'm not bragging. That is just a fact!

"Would you like to know the secret to glowing, super-smooth skin?

"It's Crème Secrète—made with all-natural ingredients."

But after the opening, Nancy and Bree got into another argument. Nancy wanted to say, "Apply at night before bedtime. You'll see amazing results the very next morning! That's a promise—a guarantee."

Bree wouldn't hear of that. "We just made this stuff. We don't know if it really works. That's false advertising." Bree was very strict about sticking to the whole truth and nothing but the truth.

"Okay. Okay." Nancy thought for a moment. Then she said, "How about this . . . 'Apply every night before bedtime. We are almost positive—that's nearly a hundred percent sure—that you'll see results pretty soon.'"

"That's better."

Nancy and Bree flipped a coin to see who

would be the actress in the commercial. Nancy won. She dressed up in a fancy nightgown of Bree's. Then she added a boa just for fun.

"Okay. Action!" Bree said once she borrowed her mother's smartphone.

Nancy got through the first part perfectly. After smearing on Crème Secrète, she yawned and pretended to fall asleep in Bree's bed. She snored to make it seem more authentic, more real.

Then Bree announced off-camera, "It's morning now. So let's see if Crème Secrète worked."

At that moment Nancy sat up and

grabbed a mirror that they'd put on the night table.

"Ooh la la!" Nancy said, peering at her reflection. "I look so young!"

Unfortunately, Bree had to keep filming the commercial over and over because every time Nancy got to that part, she burst out laughing.

Bree was getting irritated.

"Sorry," Nancy said. "It's just that old people want to look younger. Nine-year-olds don't. We want to look older."

So they switched and Nancy filmed Bree. No

surprise—Bree went through the whole thing perfectly the first time.

"It's a superb commercial," Nancy said.

"But you really think people are going to buy Crème Secrète? Your dad said he will, and maybe Mrs. DeVine will to be nice. But will anybody else?"

Nancy was wiping the last of the cream off her face. Bree had a point. "Yeah . . . plus it was fun making it once, but I wouldn't want to keep making lots more." Nancy sniffed and made a face. "It smells a little funny. Doesn't it? I think maybe we put in too much cinnamon."

By then it was time for Nancy to leave. So they said *au revoir* and Nancy took a jar of Crème Secrète home with her. She gave it to her dad for free. He dabbed some on his face. His nose wrinkled. Nancy could tell her father thought it smelled weird too.

Still, Crème Secrète turned out to be a big hit with someone in the family . . .

Frenchy!

The next morning the jar was empty. Somehow Frenchy had managed to get the top off. She'd licked up every bit of Crème Secrète.

CHAPTER 7

THE BUN CROWN

t didn't take long for Nancy and Bree to follow another path on the road to riches.

Tuesday afternoon Bree came clickety-clacketing in her tap shoes over to Nancy's right after her dance class.

"I know how we're going to get rich!

"Look at this picture I took on my mom's

cell. It's a little girl in beginner ballet." Bree handed the phone to Nancy. The photo

showed a girl around JoJo's age whose hair was in a bun on top of her head. Around the bun was a tiny gold tiara.

"Adorable!" Nancy said.

"I thought of a name already. We can call it the Bun Crown," Bree said.

"The Bun Crown." Nancy repeated the name out loud. Yes, it was perfect.

"It'll be easy-peasy to make them." Bree had figured that out on the car ride home. "We can cut crowns out of cardboard and cover them with gold foil from the chocolate. Then all we need to do is punch in holes for ribbons to tie on the crowns."

"Wow, you've thought of everything," Nancy said. She couldn't help feeling a little disappointed in herself. Maybe Bree had more entrepreneurial spirit than she did.

❖ ❖ ❖

On Saturday Bree and Nancy began Bun Crown production. They worked on the tool table in Bree's garage. They decided that their first sample looked too plain. So they stuck on fancy jewel stickers and—*voilà*—gorgeous Bun Crowns!

After Bree bribed Nancy's sister with a Solid Gold chocolate bar, JoJo agreed to model the Bun Crown. The photo of her came out a little blurry. But JoJo wouldn't sit still for a retake. Instead she zipped outside to play in Bree's yard with Freddy.

While they were making an ad, Bree's dad came into the garage. He picked up a Bun Crown and read their ad. He thought it looked very professional.

"I'm going to ask Mom to put it up on her Facebook page."

"I like the slogan," Bree's dad said.

"I came up with that," Nancy told him.

The Bun Crown
What's très fancy and fun?
A crown for your bun!
Be the first on your block to wear one!

Soon Nancy had to leave. Andy was coming over for her guitar lesson. Bree gave her a sample to take home.

"The Bun Crown! We're going to make millions," Nancy said. Then they squealed, hugged each other, and squealed some more.

CHAPTER 8

THE BEST THINGS IN LIFE ARE FREE?

Andy taught Nancy a new song that afternoon. The name of it was "The Best Things in Life Are Free."

"The chords aren't that hard."

Sure enough, after a while Nancy was able to strum along while Andy sang.

"The moon belongs to everyone.

"The best things in life are free.

"The stars belong to everyone.

"They gleam there for you and me."

It surprised Nancy that Andy had picked this song to teach her. The songs he liked best had a hard, pounding beat. Rock classics like "Wild Thing" and "Louie Louie." This song was very different. It was sweet and slow and old-fashioned.

"My band's got a gig tonight," Andy explained. "Friends of my grandparents are celebrating their fiftieth wedding anniversary. This is the song they want at the end of the party."

He made Nancy play it a few more times. Then they took a break.

Over a glass of lemonade, Nancy thought more about the words to the song. Of course the moon and stars were free. All you had to do was look up in the sky to see them. "Do you think the lyrics make sense? About the best things being free?"

"Dunno." Andy drained his glass. "I never really thought about it."

Neither had Nancy. Not until now.

"You're an entrepreneur, Andy. Making money is important to you, right?"

"Most definitely."

"You love playing guitar. But would you give lessons for free?" Nancy asked.

"Listen. You're an amazingly cool kid, and it's fun teaching you guitar. But no. I wouldn't be doing it for free. I need to make money."

Nancy poured more lemonade for him. "Are you saving up for something extra-special?"

"Sure am. It's called college. I'll be going in two years and my parents can't afford to pay for all of it. So I'm saving as much as I can to help out."

Back in the living room, Nancy spent the rest of the lesson going over the song

Andy had taught her last time—"Rock Around the Clock." Practicing had paid off, because twice Andy said, "Sweet!"

Just before he left, JoJo came bursting into the living room. She still had on her crown. "Help! The king is after me!"

A moment later Freddy appeared. He had on a towel cape and—Nancy noticed—a Bun Crown too. Only his was taped to his head. One of the points was already ripped off.

Freddy started chasing JoJo around the sofa until Nancy yelled, "Halt!" She turned to Freddy. "Did Bree say you could have that crown?"

Freddy didn't answer. He looked sideways at JoJo.

"JoJo, you gave it to Freddy, didn't you? Without asking."

JoJo didn't answer either. Instead, she hopped onto Andy's lap and said, "Nancy made this." She lowered her head so he could see the crown.

"Very cute," Andy said.

"It's a Bun Crown," JoJo went on. "It's Nancy and Bree's business. They want to be millionaires. Nancy is going to take me to Paris."

Nancy scowled. Yes, she'd said that. But

it sounded silly, hearing JoJo say it.

Then JoJo pulled off her crown, handed it to Andy, and said, "Want to buy it?"

"Andy, don't listen to JoJo—"

"No, wait." Andy examined the crown. "This is cute. And it's my little cousin's

birthday in a couple of weeks. How much is it?"

"It's a dollar ninety-nine," Nancy said shyly. "But honestly don't feel like you have to buy one."

Andy insisted, and after placing two brand-new dollar bills in Nancy's hand, he packed up his guitar and took off.

"Wait." Nancy followed after him. "I forgot! I owe you a penny."

Andy was already out the front door. He didn't even turn around. With a backward wave, he told Nancy to keep the change and jumped into his truck.

So Nancy double-backed to the kitchen and ran out the side door. Wait till she handed Bree one of the two crisp bills. It was beyond thrilling, even if she did have

to thank her little sister for it.

Maybe, just maybe, the Bun Crown *was*
going to make them millionaires!

CHAPTER 9

BUSINESS TROUBLES

The ad for the Bun Crown went up on Facebook, and soon twelve orders had come in.

Unfortunately, there were problems. After making more crowns, Bree ran out of the gold-foil chocolate-bar wrappers.

"Can't your dad get more?" Nancy asked.

"Nope. But I bet we can find gold foil—or something just like it—at the crafts store."

Problem solved!

After lunch on Saturday, Nancy's dad took them downtown. Between them, Nancy and Bree had seven dollars and change. That also was a problem. The supplies at the crafts store came to over eleven dollars. Eleven dollars and eighteen cents, to be exact.

"Um, Dad, could we borrow three dollars and—" Nancy paused to count up all their coins. "Um . . . actually, maybe four dollars?"

"Ladies, you caught me at just the right moment. I've been searching for a growth opportunity like the Bun Crown to invest in."

Nancy had no idea what her dad was

talking about. Still, she figured the answer was yes since he took out his wallet.

"Thanks, Dad. We'll pay you back as soon as we get paid for the twelve orders."

An hour later, the girls had everything set up again on the work table in Bree's garage. Bree wrote a list of people who had ordered the Bun Crown. As soon as they finished making one, Bree checked off a name.

"We are so professional!" Nancy said, and they high-fived each other.

After an hour of Bun Crown production, however, there was yet another problem. They had no more jewel stickers.

So it was back to the crafts store, this time with Bree's mom, who loaned them more money. The Gem Brite stickers the girls had been using cost three dollars a package. There were cheaper jewel stickers for sale but Bree and Nancy agreed that only the finest would do for the Bun Crowns.

By the end of the afternoon, twelve

golden, bejeweled Bun Crowns gleamed before them. As soon as they finished, they presented one to Mrs. DeVine, who had bought a Bun Crown for Jewel. Since no parent was free to chauffeur them around town, Nancy and Bree had to wait until Sunday to make all the deliveries.

All their customers were delighted with the Bun Crowns and every single person insisted on the girls keeping the change when they tried to hand over a penny. Bree and Nancy arrived back at the club with a stack of dollar bills. A real wad of money. Altogether they had made twenty-four dollars. Nancy couldn't take her eyes off it. "We are going to be rich, rich, rich." She pictured herself gazing down on Paris from the top of the Eiffel Tower.

"Remember, we still have to pay our parents back," Bree said.

Nancy wished Bree hadn't brought that up so soon. "I know. But before we do, let's look at all our cash a little while longer."

Sadly, after repaying the loans, the pile of dollar bills had dwindled. That meant it was much, much smaller. Their expenses had added up to a lot more than either Nancy or Bree had realized. If they counted in the money of their own that they'd spent, all that was left over was

three dollars and twelve cents. And that was going to be split between them.

Nancy, discouraged, blew out through her lips. "I can't believe it. So much hard work and only a dollar and fifty-six cents for each of us." She tried looking on the bright side. At least now they had enough supplies to make lots more Bun Crowns. So when more orders came in, the money would be all theirs.

"I think maybe we made a mistake with the price," Bree decided. "It was way too low. If we had charged two ninety-nine, we would have made so much more money."

Nancy sighed. "Why didn't we figure that out sooner?" Forget about getting rich quick—they weren't even getting rich slowly.

CHAPTER 10

ANTIQUES IN YOUR ATTIC

On Wednesday, Nancy's class got to watch a movie, an educational kind called a documentary. That meant nothing in it was made up. This one was about the Gold Rush. Near the end, photos of miners in long beards and dirty clothes flashed, one after another, on the screen while an actor off camera read aloud a letter. It had been written by a miner to his wife. He was miserable!

"With the money I laid out for equipment and paying rent to sleep in a tent, I'm poorer now than before."

The miner had staked a claim. That meant he—and nobody else—could look for gold in a certain plot of land. It had cost him a lot to get the claim. And it was all for nothing.

"I have not struck gold, although a fellow nearby did. Nuggets the size of peas. He's rich. Yet I have nothing to show. I am so

sorry to have let down you and the little ones. I thought I would have a fortune by now."

Nancy knew how the prospector felt! Of course, she didn't have a family to support. And she had made a little money. But although Bree checked every day on Facebook, no new orders had come in for the Bun Crown. Nancy found it a little hard hearing how wealthy other kids were getting.

Clara was making a bundle from her biscuit stand. One day she came in wearing silver sequined sneakers. "I bought them with money from my biscuit business."

Mr. Dudeny had overheard Clara. "It sounds like your idea is really taking off."

Clara beamed.

Later, Mr. D. asked Clara to tell the class more about her business. He didn't have to remind her this time about speaking loud and proud.

"I started out selling biscuits from a stand in front of my house," she said. "But now people are calling and placing orders. One lady ordered two dozen."

Mr. Dudeny explained that Clara was successful because "there is a demand for the product she's selling—great homemade biscuits."

Robert was also making lots of money teaching lasso tricks. He had five students coming once a week for three dollars an hour.

"How is the way Robert is earning money different from Clara?"

Right away, Clara said, "I'm biscuits and he's lassos."

Mr. Dudeny didn't seem entirely satisfied with that answer. "Anything else that makes their businesses different?"

Nancy cupped her hand in her chin and pondered. She thought about her guitar teacher, Andy. Then, since nobody else's hand was up, she raised hers. "Well, Clara is making something. Robert isn't. He's teaching something he's good at."

"Exactly!" Mr. Dudeny said. "Clara is providing a product and Robert is offering a service. They are two different types of businesses. So, Robert and Clara, are there downsides to being successful and making money?"

Nancy was surprised when both of

them shouted, "Yes!"

Robert said that he used to relax after school by playing video games for an hour. "Now with my lasso classes, I can't."

"And I missed my little cousin's birthday party because of that big biscuit order that came in last Sunday," Clara said.

Mr. Dudeny nodded. "Robert and Clara both have had to give up some fun, some leisure time. Being an entrepreneur is hard work."

"You can say that again," Robert said.

It turned out that Lionel was one of Robert's new students. As soon as the last bell rang, he came over to Nancy and asked, "Is it okay if we cancel checkers today?" Lionel and Nancy had a weekly after-school game. "Robert has to go to the dentist after school tomorrow. So he wants to switch my lesson to today."

"Okay," Nancy replied, a little disappointed. Then she and Bree hopped on their bikes and rode off. Since there was no homework for tomorrow, they decided to hang out in their clubhouse and read the latest Nancy Drew books that they'd checked out from the library.

"We're not rich. But we certainly have plenty of leisure time," Nancy pointed out.

Just as they turned onto their block, they saw Mrs. DeVine standing by the front gate to her house. The moment she spotted Nancy and Bree, she started waving frantically. Jewel was yipping and racing around her ankles.

"You'll never guess!" Mrs. DeVine said. "A

week from Sunday, *Antiques in Your Attic* is coming to town! They're taping a show."

Nancy and Bree were way more than surprised. They were flabbergasted.

"I've been checking the show's website every day. Today they just put up the schedule of cities for the new season. We'll be one of the first shows on air."

Nancy and Bree stared at each other. They both knew what the other was thinking. Nancy Drew could wait. This called for tea!

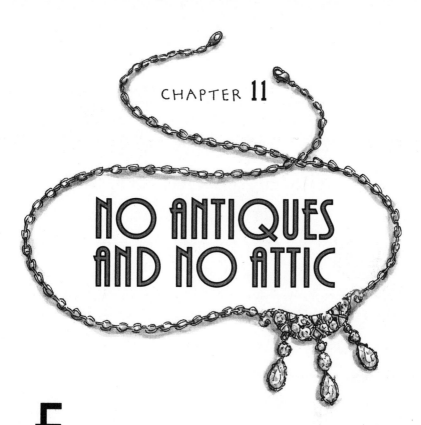

CHAPTER 11

NO ANTIQUES AND NO ATTIC

Five minutes later, Nancy was sipping mint tea from a china cup. It was part of Mrs. DeVine's best tea set, with tiny blue flowers. There was a matching teapot, a pitcher for cream, and a sugar bowl with tiny silver tongs for picking up sugar cubes. "You should bring the tea set to

Antiques in Your Attic," Nancy suggested.

"And that too." Bree was pointing at a silver tray with slices of cake on it. Mrs. DeVine's initials were engraved on the tray. Her initials from her first marriage.

"I plan to do a thorough search of the attic," Mrs. DeVine told the girls. "I've forgotten half of what's up there. Mostly junk, but you never know."

Nancy had little doubt that Mrs. DeVine would turn up some antiques. It was going to be harder finding anything valuable at the Clancy home. The Clancys didn't even have an attic to search through. At dinner that night, Nancy asked, "Do we own any antiques?"

The answer (as she figured) was no.

Nancy told her mom and dad about

the TV show coming to the arena outside of town. "It doesn't even have to be an antique. Something rare would be good. Something that's one of a kind."

"Rare and one of a kind? You're looking right at her." Then Nancy's dad leaned

over to kiss her mother.

"Be serious, Dad. Mrs. DeVine is going to take Bree and me to the show and I need to bring interesting stuff."

"Okay. What about my comic books? I've always wondered what they're worth."

"Superb."

"And that poster." Her mother pointed to the one in the den. Nancy knew it was from a rock concert that her parents had gone to on their first date. The band was called Pearl Jam. "That might be worth something."

While they were clearing the table, the phone rang.

It was Bree.

"I started writing you a secret message, but it was taking way too long. Have you looked for antiques yet?" Bree didn't wait for an answer. Instead, she started telling Nancy what she was bringing.

"Vintage perfume bottles from the nineteen twenties and thirties."

Nancy knew the ones Bree meant. They sat on Bree's mother's dressing table. Nancy also knew, from watching the show, that vintage meant almost an antique.

"And," Bree went on, "my mom has her grandpa's army uniform with his canteen and dog tags."

"Oh, you're so lucky!" Nancy tried

not to feel jealous. "They love old soldier stuff."

After dinner Nancy searched through her house. Besides the poster and comic books, she decided on a green vase with red dots. It looked like it had measles. But often really ugly vases ended up being worth a lot.

What also turned up was the teardrop necklace. It was on the floor of the den by an armchair. Nancy blinked. For a moment she thought she must be looking at a twin of the one she was wearing. Then her hand flew to her throat. No necklace! *Sacre bleu!* It had fallen off again.

This time Nancy's mother did not try to repair it herself. She took it to a jewelry store and a few days later, they picked it up.

"This necklace is so pretty," the man behind the counter said. He slipped it into a little Ziploc bag. "And with this new clasp, you can feel safe wearing it for another fifty, sixty years."

Nancy giggled. In sixty years, she'd be older than Mrs. DeVine!

CHAPTER 12

SHOWTIME!

When school let out on Friday, Bree and Nancy asked who was planning to go to the arena the next day.

"What for?" Nola and couple of other kids asked.

Nancy and Bree turned to each other. They were shocked. Hardly anybody knew about *Antiques in Your Attic* coming to town to film a show. And hardly anybody was interested.

"Oh, that's the show my grandpa watches. Bo-ring!" Grace said.

"No, it's not! Bree and I are going and I bet we'll have a thrilling time," Nancy insisted.

"My house is filled with antiques. They're in every room," Grace went on.

"Do you have an antique toilet?" Lionel wanted to know.

"I mean, duh. Of course not." Then Grace turned back to Nancy. "I might let you take in something of mine if you don't have any stuff that's worth money."

"I have plenty of stuff. I don't need yours," Nancy replied.

That evening her father picked out his ten best comic books. Her mom rolled up the Pearl Jam poster and packed the vase in Bubble Wrap. Later on, Nancy and Bree sent many messages back and forth discussing what to wear. They wanted to look grown-up. Mature. Nancy ended up deciding on a purple smock dress she'd worn to her cousin's bar mitzvah. And of course the teardrop necklace.

The next morning on the dot of seven, Mrs. DeVine picked up the girls. Half an hour later they joined a long line that inched toward the entrance to the arena. Thousands of people had shown up. There were people carrying rugs and tables and lamps. Old sofas and armchairs; dolls and dollhouses, paintings—lots of them—

and statues of all sizes. One family lugged in an elephant made entirely of white string. It was almost the size of a real elephant. It barely fit through the door.

Mrs. DeVine laughed. "Oh lord, an actual white elephant." A white elephant, she explained, was something very rare but totally useless. "Where do you suppose they keep it?" Then she winced and rubbed

the back of her foot. "Whatever possessed me to wear high heels?"

It took over two hours just to reach the entrance to the arena. Inside, they could see huge signs for different categories— Jewelry, Musical Instruments, Furniture, and many more. The signs hung like flags from the ceiling, and under each one sat an appraiser, someone who knew all about that category and could tell how much each person's stuff was worth. Nancy recognized several of the appraisers from watching the show.

"Over there. Under Toys," she exclaimed.

"It's the man with the ponytail who always wears a giant bow tie." Sure enough, he was wearing one that day.

Once they were inside the arena, guys in red T-shirts that said *Antiques in Your Attic* stopped each person. They took a quick look at what everyone had brought in and steered them to the right line.

"More lines!" wailed Mrs. DeVine.

Bree was sent to the Military Items, Mrs. DeVine to China and Silverware, and Nancy to Pop Culture. Nancy was about to give Mrs. DeVine the vase with measles but one of the guys in the T-shirt said, in a nice way, "You needn't bother."

Oh! So the measles vase was just plain ugly. Not ugly and valuable.

"We'll call each other every ten minutes

to stay in touch," Mrs. DeVine reminded the girls. Then they showed her that their cell phones were fully charged and listed Mrs. DeVine's phone number.

The Pop Culture line was fun. Behind Nancy were a father and his son. They had a bunch of movie posters from old horror

movies. *Creature from the Black Lagoon.* *I Was a Teenage Werewolf. Night of the Living Dead.* It was lucky Bree wasn't on this line. She couldn't stand the sight of anything bloody or gruesome.

Nancy showed them her rock-concert poster and the ten comic books. "Cool!" the dad said. But Nancy could tell he wasn't impressed. Neither was the appraiser.

"I'm afraid that the concert poster has just sentimental value for your parents," he said. "And some of the comic books"— the man was leafing through one about Superman—"well, if they were in better condition, then maybe . . ." He stopped talking because another appraiser showed up needing to speak to him. She was holding a Minnie Mouse watch. Nancy recognized her too because on TV she always looked like a walking jewelry store. She wore necklaces, tiaras, earrings, bracelets, and pins. Why, there were even pins on the back of her dress.

While the two appraisers whispered over bent heads, Nancy texted Mrs. DeVine to say she was done. After that, Nancy wasn't sure where to go. She already knew her stuff wasn't valuable. Should she leave the Pop Culture table? She fiddled with her necklace nervously. Finally she said, "Thank you very much for your expertise." Then she quickly gathered up the comic books and concert poster.

The lady with the Minnie Mouse watch suddenly glanced up and said, "No. Don't go. Wait a moment, please."

It took a moment for Nancy to realize that the lady was speaking to her.

"I noticed your pendant. May I have a closer look at it?" the lady asked.

Nancy blinked. "You mean my necklace?"

Yes. That was what the lady wanted to see. And she looked very interested!

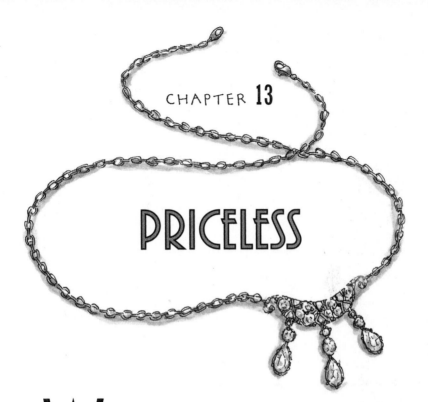

CHAPTER 13

PRICELESS

While Nancy unhooked the brand-new clasp on her necklace, she said, "Um—these aren't real diamonds. They're rhinestones. This is costume jewelry."

The appraiser smiled and took the necklace. "Yes, I know that. My specialty is costume jewelry."

A long chain she wore had a gold-rimmed magnifying glass attached to it. She peered through it at the back of Nancy's necklace.

"Yes! Just as I hoped." She showed Nancy that two tiny letters were stamped on the back: *BL*. "It stands for Babette Labelle. The costume jewelry she designed was very popular in the nineteen forties and fifties."

Double ooh la la! This was exciting news. Her necklace was made by someone famous, someone who sounded French!

"Was the necklace made in Paris?" Nancy asked.

"Oh, no. The factory was in Brooklyn. Babette Labelle wasn't the designer's real name. She was born Barbara Levine.

She was a housewife who liked making jewelry. And one day she just decided she was going into business."

"So she was an entrepreneur!"

"Very much so. The company was very successful, but closed after her death in the nineteen eighties. Lately there has been renewed interest in Babette Labelle jewelry. This piece is smaller than her most famous pieces. One necklace looks like a waterfall of rhinestones. It would practically come down to your waist." The lady turned the necklace right side up again. "Nevertheless, this is lovely and I'd venture to say that it's worth about two hundred dollars."

Two hundred dollars! Two hundred dollars was a fortune!

Nancy stood with her mouth open like a fish. She could feel her eyes bugging out. When she finally could speak, she said exactly what everybody on the show always said: "Wow! That is amazing! I had no idea!"

The lady returned the necklace. Nancy's hands were trembling so much, she needed help putting it back on.

"If you ever want to part with your pendant, ask your parents to find out what shops in the area sell vintage costume jewelry. I'm sure one of them would want to buy your pendant."

"Oh, I would never sell it. But *merci! Merci beaucoup!*" Nancy told the lady, and said good-bye.

Out of the corner of her eye, she saw

Mrs. DeVine and Bree rushing toward her from across the hall. Nancy raced to meet them.

Bree grabbed both of Nancy's hands. She started hopping up and down. "Nancy, Nancy!" she screamed. "My army stuff is worth two hundred and fifty dollars!"

"My necklace is worth two hundred!" Suddenly saying that made it seem real. Nancy started screaming too. And they didn't stop until one of the TV people came over and asked them to lower their voices.

So on the car ride home they filled each other in and screamed as much as they wanted.

It turned out that Bree's great-grandfather had joined the army in a special year, 1948. Bree now knew that was the first time black and white soldiers lived together in the army. Before, they'd been kept separate. "The picture of my great-grandpa in his uniform—along with the actual uniform—makes my stuff a historical collection!"

Then Nancy explained how just by accident she found out about her necklace. "Only, the lady kept calling it a pendant."

From the backseat Nancy asked Mrs. DeVine, "Did you know it was made by a jewelry designer named Babette Labelle? She was pretty famous in the nineteen fifties."

"No, I didn't." Mrs. DeVine made a left onto their street. "But I'm awfully glad you both made out better than I did. The tea set is a copy of very valuable china made in England, and the silver tray turned out to be only silver plated." She pulled to a stop. "Oh well. I am no richer than when we started out this morning. But I'm no poorer either."

Later, after they calmed down, Nancy and Bree went to the clubhouse to discuss their good fortune.

"Of course, the army stuff doesn't even belong to me—it belongs to my mom. She'd never sell it, and—" Bree thought for a moment. "I wouldn't ever want her to."

Nancy nodded. "I will never sell the neck—I mean, the pendant." Nancy loved Mrs. DeVine. Having something special of hers, Nancy realized, meant way more than the money it was worth. To Nancy, the pendant was priceless.

CHAPTER 14

STARRY NIGHT

t was an unusually mild night. So the Clancys ate dinner at the picnic table in their backyard. For dessert, they invited over Bree's family and Mrs. DeVine.

"Look!" Her dad pointed up at the sky. "Have you ever seen so many stars?"

Nancy looked up. He was right. The

131

sky was studded with stars—bazillions of them—and they seemed to be twinkling even brighter than usual. Nancy searched for all the constellations she knew. Then she and Bree made up their own constellations.

"There's one group of stars that looks like the Eiffel Tower," Nancy said, pointing.

Her mom was sitting next to her on the picnic bench. She slung her arm around Nancy and said, "You'll get to the real Eiffel Tower one day. Of that I am sure, Mademoiselle Clancy."

Nancy leaned back against her mom. Nobody had a better smell than her mother, who didn't even wear perfume. They stared up at the sky together for a while, and suddenly Nancy remembered a line from the song Andy had taught her.

The stars really did belong to everyone.

She ran to the house, went upstairs to her room, and got her guitar.

When she returned to the yard, Nancy began playing for everyone. Maybe what the song said was true. Maybe the best things in life were free.

A CHAPTER BOOK SERIES
 STARRING EVERYONE'S
FAVORITE FANCY GIRL

HARPER
An Imprint of HarperCollinsPublishers

www.fancynancyworld.com